For Mum. Thank you.
—R.S.

Splat and the New Baby
Copyright © 2018 by Rob Scotton
www.harpercollinschildrens.com
ISBN 978-0-06-213389-2
Typography by Jeanne L. Hogle
18 19 20 21 22   PC   10 9 8 7 6 5 4 3 2
❖
First Edition

# Splat

## and the
## New Baby

# Rob Scotton

**HARPER**

*An Imprint of HarperCollinsPublishers*

Splat's eyes widened and his mouth fell open when his mom told him the news.

"Soon, Splat, there's going to be a new baby in the house."

"This is FANTASTIC news!"
cheered Splat.

"Hmm, and that means
there's a lot to do."

"I'm going to need a little help.

"DAD!"

Splat decorated the nursery.
Dad helped a little.

Splat fetched his old crib from the basement.
Dad helped a little.

Dad had been a big help.
"Good job, Dad!"

Later Splat was thinking up
more things to do, when his
Dad said . . .

"Splat, Mom will be home
soon with a baby . . ."

But before Dad could finish
what he was saying, the front
gate squeaked open.

"Wow! The new baby's here!"
cried Splat.

Splat leaped from his room . . .

raced across the landing . . .

Splat turned the latch and opened the door.

He looked up at his mom and smiled.

He looked down at the new baby and . . .

Splat spun around . . .

skidded across the hall . . .

slid up the stair rail . . .

raced across the landing . . .
leaped into his room . . .

and shut the door with a . . . SLAM!

Splat couldn't believe what he'd seen.

"The new baby . . .

is . . .

a . . .

"His name is Urgle," said Splat's dad.

"And he's staying with us while his mom is away on a trip."

"And I promise he won't eat us all up."

"Urgle doesn't have any brothers and sisters," Dad explained.
"Maybe you could treat Urgle like your own little brother?"

Splat thought for a while.

It's impossible . . .

Or is it?

And then he said . . .

"I'll do my best!"

Maybe . . .

"Mom, since Urgle doesn't have any
brothers or sisters, can I be his big brother?"

"That's a great idea," said his mom.

Urgle

"Maybe you could help Urgle at . . .

"Mealtimes?"
"I'll do my best!"

"Bath times?"
"I'll do my best!"

"Bedtimes?"
"I'll do my best!"

"Diaper-changing times?"

Urgle

Splat introduced himself.
"Hello Urgle, I'm Splat, and I'm going to be your big brother."

Urgle

Over the next few days . . .

At mealtimes . . .

Splat did his best.

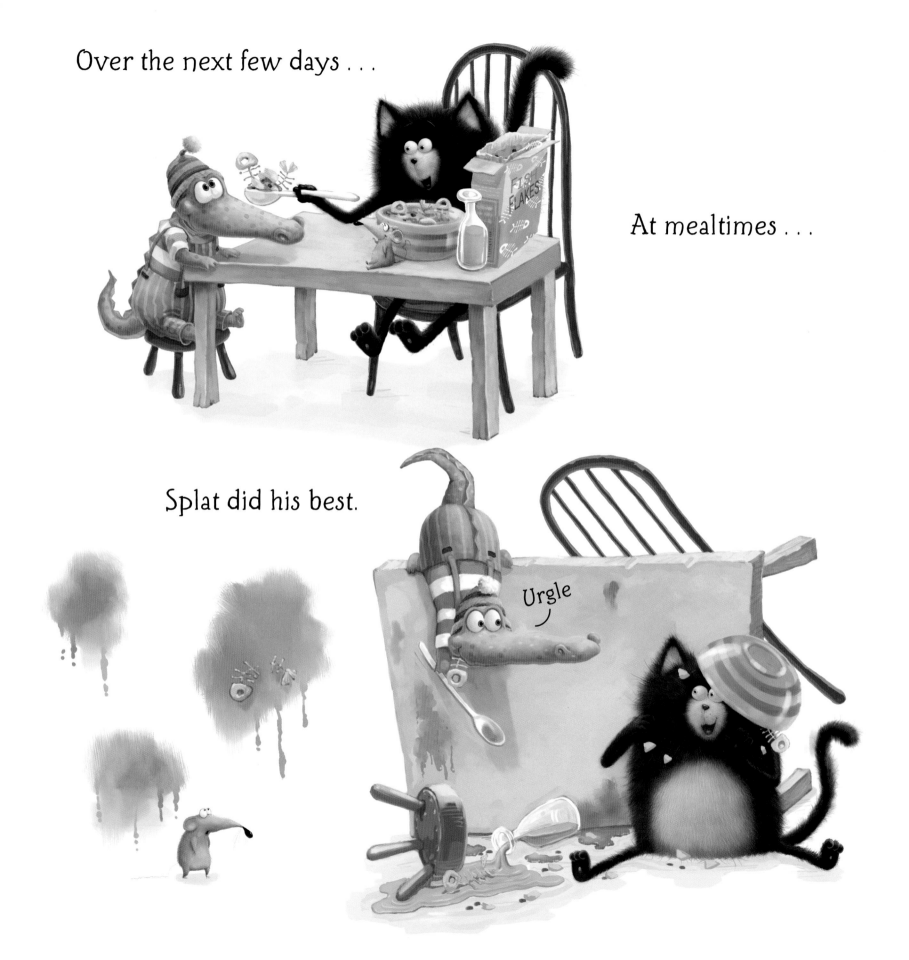

Urgle

At bath times . . .

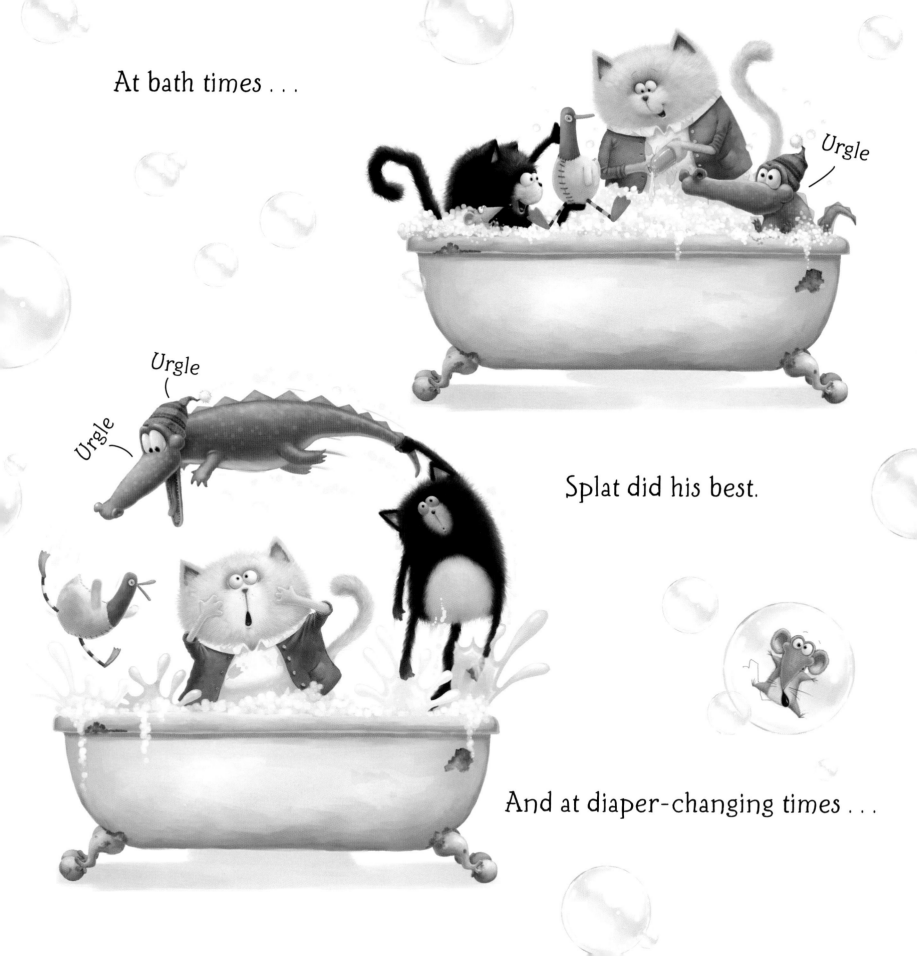

Urgle

Urgle

Urgle

Urgle

Splat did his best.

And at diaper-changing times . . .

Even then, Splat did his best.

Splat especially loved bedtime,
when he read all his favorite stories to Urgle.

Urgle

All too soon it was time for
Urgle to go home.
"I'll visit whenever I can,"
said Splat.

Urgle

"Bye, Urgle!"

Plat . . . Plat . . . Plat . . .

"Splat, you have been an amazing big brother," said his mom.

"And when will I be a big brother again?" asked Splat.

"One day soon," said his mom.

"One day VERY soon."